First published 2023

EK Books
an imprint of Exisle Publishing Pty Ltd
PO Box 864, Chatswood, NSW 2057, Australia
226 High Street, Dunedin, 9016, New Zealand
www.exislepublishing.com

A CiP record for this book is available from the National Library of Australia.

ISBN 978-1-922539-39-7

Designed by Mark Thacker
Typeset in Minion Pro 13 on 22pt
Printed in China

This book uses paper sourced under ISO 14001 guidelines from well-managed forests and other controlled sources.

10 9 8 7 6 5 4 3 2 1

GAME ON!

SHRINKLE

EMILY SNAPE

Book 2 in the 'Game On' series!

Available late 2023

For Barnaby. Thank you for all the little things *and* the big things in our lives.

LEVEL
ONE

Spider breath smells worse than rotten eggs.

I know this for a fact because last night, Liam and I made the most mind blowing *and dangerous* discovery of our lives …

Probably in the **entire history of the universe**.

It's called … **SHRINKLE**. And it all began when I followed Liam to the loo.

But let me just rewind time a bit, to give you all the facts. (I really like facts, that's something you should know about me.)

FRIDAY AFTERNOON, 3.43 P.M.
COUNTDOWN TIMER: 137 MINUTES

So, before Shrinkle flipped everything inside out, my day had already been going seriously wrong. It was, in fact, the **most embarrassing day of my life**.

Mr Vipond, our teacher, had got us to spend the afternoon rearranging random words into their correct alphabetical order.

B ... Be
B ... Boring?
C ... Could
M ... More
T ... This

It had felt like the longest two hours of my life, but eventually I completed the list and he said I could spend the last ten minutes of school on my spring project. I'd been working on it for weeks and it was almost finished …

In the main hall I'd created a huge timeline tracking 'The Evolution of the Video Game'. I'd sketched a picture of the first ever game, invented in 1958. It was called 'Tennis for Two' and it was basically two lines and a circle. (How did they survive back then?)

The final section of the display was going to be what I thought the future of gaming *might* look like. I'd spent ages last night drawing a diagram of a TOTALLY EPIC, fully immersive VR body suit.

I zipped open my backpack to fish it out.

But instead of my art folder, my bag was stuffed with **balled up clothing**. Confused, I yanked it all out, searching for my work … before I realized … the material was all PANTS. Not just one pair … I'd pulled out hundreds of UNDERPANTS!

Baggy ones. Lacy ones. Even ones with little unicorns leaping all over them.

My bag had been stuffed to the brim. And now they

were all over my desk.

I'd been pranked. *And I know EXACTLY who by,* I thought. It could only have been my INFURIATING brother, Liam: self-proclaimed **King of Pranks**.

With trembling hands, I started to shove the pants back in my bag, but before I could manage, Min (the loudest girl in my class) had noticed.

'Er ... are you sure you've got enough pants there, Max?' she hooted. Everyone turned to look.

My face went as red as Sonic the Hedgehog's shoes, but thankfully the bell rang for the end of school so I shot straight out of there.

Panting ... (scratch that, no more *pant* talk, please) ... *Gasping* for breath, I ran as fast as I could towards home, my head in a loop of Min's sneering expression and the class jeering at me.

I couldn't believe what had just happened. I wasn't even going to be able to yell at Liam. (I couldn't give him the satisfaction of knowing that his stupid prank had

worked. But I was going to get my own back. Somehow.)

At least I wouldn't have to face my brother this evening.

I had the perfect Friday night ahead of me. I'd been planning it ALL week and I didn't want anything to ruin it, even this. I would just have to put Liam and Min and embarrassing underwear out of my mind.

I started humming my favourite video game soundtrack loudly to myself and focused on my four-stage plan. I had every detail worked out:

1. Go home to an empty flat.

    Mum was working late. Clio, my bonkers baby sister, was booked in at her child minder's. But best of all, my brother was going straight after school to a sleepover.

    For once, Mum wouldn't be hassling me to do something other than play computer games and the tiny bedroom I shared with my brother would be ALL MINE! There would be NO Liam thinking I'd be impressed by an odd-shaped bogey that *he* thought looked like Yoda or pestering me to attempt an obstacle course he'd created out of MY stuff.

2. Throw off my itchy school uniform the moment I was home.

   Okay, not actually *in the* doorway — I wasn't revealing **any more** pants today. Just as soon as I got to my bedroom. Then, get changed straight away into my super-soft gaming PJs. They might be old and have a few holes in embarrassing places (Mum keeps trying to throw them out), but they are SO comfy.

3. Make myself a **KS**

   Here's the recipe for a PERFECT **K**etchup **S**andwich: Bread. Ketchup. More ketchup. Another couple of squirts … and then bread. Mum always tries to sneak cucumber or carrots in, *like I wouldn't notice*, so I only really get to scoff them when she's at work.

4. Finally crack the computer game I've been trying to smash for the last THREE WEEKS.
   No interruptions. Just me and my PC and the whole evening stretching gloriously ahead of me. Perfect.

As I turned the corner of my street, the memory of the horrific afternoon fading away like a bad dream, someone suddenly grabbed my arm.

I spun around and my heart sank to the bottom of my sneakers.

It was **Min**.

Okay, so, quick quiz. If this happened to you, would you:

a. Smile in a non-geeky way and say, 'Oh hi, Min. Up to anything good at the weekend?' like the whole *pants* thing had never happened.

b. Say something clever AND believable to explain the pants fiasco that didn't make you sound insane.

c. Do neither of the above and instead just stand there, stuttering. Maybe even splutter a bit. Basically, start glitching in real life.

Well, no prizes for guessing what *I* did.

(Why did I freeze? That NEVER happens to me when I'm gaming.)

Min smirked and said, 'Hey, Pants-Face! Why can't you be more like your brother … he's a LEGEND! His latest prank, the emails … Genius!'

UGGGHHHHH! What else has Liam been up to? I thought.

I don't know if I explained properly, but Liam is my younger brother. In the entire history **of the world**, younger brothers are NEVER cooler than older brothers.

It's against natural law. I don't know how he does it but somehow everyone thinks Liam is awesome … and I'm the only one who can see him for what he is. A total banana brain who's ruining my life. (Fact: humans share 60 per cent of their DNA with bananas. With Liam, it is at least 99.5 per cent.)

He's definitely NO genius. Would a genius have a terrible catchphrase? No, of course not. Einstein was a genius. He didn't have a catch phrase. Liam, on the other hand, does. It is INFURIATING.

When something bad has happened, Liam just shrugs and says, 'It's all good!' Honestly. He does it all the time.

Here are some examples:

ME: Liam, why have you cut your toenails on my pillow?
LIAM: It's all good!
ME: Liam, you've finished the milk.
LIAM: It's all good!

ME: Liam, humans are causing life on Earth to vanish.'

You get the idea. It is **the worst**.

The only thing that stops Liam in his tracks is spiders. He screams in fear when he spots one, even if it's just on the TV. Unfortunately, I still haven't managed to film him in full panic mode *yet*.

All I wanted to do this afternoon was relax, eat my snacks, play my game and forget all about having the WWB: **World's Worst Brother**.

But as I reached the door of my flat, I could already hear it was far from empty.

Here's what greeted me:

- Mum screaming at Liam.
- Liam yelling, full volume, back at her. (I doubt either of them could actually tell what the other was saying.)

- My baby sister wailing on top of all the noise.
- Declan, fast asleep, in the doorway, despite ALL of the chaos.

(Declan is next door's cat and he is OFFICIALLY the laziest creature alive. He should've been born a sloth. He could snooze *on* the Formula One racetrack … or even on the pitch of a World Cup final. Literally … anywhere.)

I stepped carefully over Dec and tried to dart straight past my crazy family when I heard Mum shriek, '… and the *only* person I can get to babysit is Miss McBoob.' (That's her real name, honest.)

I stopped dead in my tracks. *Miss McBoob … coming here? Noooooooo!*

'Why can't Dad come over?' Liam sulked.

'What's going on?' I asked, rolling my eyes, not really wanting to hear the answer. 'And Dad can't come over. I don't want to see him.' Miss McBoob might be certifiably mad but at least *she* hadn't deserted us.

'I thought you were working at that museum event and Liam was going to be at Taksh's house and …' I moaned.

Mum put her head in her hands. 'My job was cancelled. Apparently the museum found a bigger company who can provide cheaper food.'

'Surely they can't just do that to you, Mum?' I cried. 'You made all those tiny hamburgers last night.' (My mum cooks minute versions of everyone's favourite meals for big events. Itsy-bitsy hot dogs the size of fingernails and cupcakes smaller than pennies. The sushi is made from one grain of rice. They look cute but you do have to gobble about 43,001 to actually feel full.)

'Well, I guess you know what *you're* having for supper. One hundred and forty miniature cheeseburgers. Anyway, I couldn't have gone to work. The school just called me,' Mum replied.

Liam raised his eyebrows, in a 'who me?' expression. (Why can't I raise my eyebrows like that? When I try to do it, they go sideways rather than up. Fact: The average person has 250 hairs per eyebrow. That's five hundred hairs on MY OWN FACE that don't do what I tell them to.)

'Your brother was caught red-handed, hacking the school's database,' Mum said, letting out a long sigh. 'I have to go to an emergency meeting right now with the head teacher. Liam sent out an email from the school office to *every* parent apologizing for accidentally feeding hedgehog meatballs to their kids. And on top of everything, Clio has nits, again.'

Clio started to howl even louder and I **snapped**. This was meant to be my perfect Friday afternoon, and now look at it.

My brother had humiliated me in front of my whole class and Min, and the rest of the school was either going to be talking about **the pants** or **the emails** all weekend. It was obviously already clear to everyone that it was Liam behind it all. His pranks are famous.

Like when he hacked the school website and added tiny moustaches onto all the staff photos. Or when he got the speakers to play the theme song from *The LEGO Movie* during an exam.

Liam was Mr Pranks and now I was Mr Pants. It wasn't fair.

Unable to contain my anger, I launched myself at Liam like a tornado. Grabbing a handful of his hair in my fist, I wrestled him to the ground.

'Get off him,' Mum shrieked. 'That is **it**. *All* screen time is banned for both of you. I've had enough. I'm trying as hard as I can to keep this family going and you two … *Agghh!*' And she ran around the flat frantically grabbing all our devices.

I froze, mid-fight and watched in horror as Mum yanked out wires from our computers and shoved remote controls haphazardly under her arm.

'I'm locking these in the boot of the car,' she snarled.

'Hello, dears!' We all spun our heads around.

Miss McBoob stood in the doorway looking like … um, I actually can't think of a good comparison. She's *really* old, has fluffy blue hair and is some sort of real life, scatter-brained, mad scientist. We're always taking unusually shaped parcels in for her, and weird robotic sounds and mysterious laser beams radiate from her flat late at night. I think Mum said she used to work for NASA on extraterrestrial technology or something.

She seemed to be wearing a homemade astronaut costume with a foil leotard (that left NOTHING to the imagination — *ugh!*), hover boots and enormous head-phones made out of toilet plungers. (This is who Mum was trusting to look after us …)

'I have to run, I'm sorry Miss McBoob,' Mum said, glancing at her watch and detaching Clio from her leg. 'NO SCREEN TIME …' she bellowed at us, sprinting to the car, wires dangling wildly behind her.

'What are we meant to do then, Mum?' I shouted back.

'Play a game … How about Monopoly?' Mum's voice trailed back as she sped off towards school.

I looked at Liam with pure hatred in my eyes.

'Bagsy being the Scottie dog,' Liam smirked from underneath me. I am *always* the dog piece in Monopoly and he knows it.

'Hmmm, Monopoly? I don't know that one,' Miss McBoob mused, closing the door behind her and pulling on thick, light-up goggles. I rolled my eyes. This was going to be a long afternoon.

Well, you can imagine how playing a board game with officially the biggest cheat in the world *and* an insane neighbour turned out. Yup, it was a disaster. It took us HONESTLY twenty minutes to agree on who would get to roll the dice first. Then:

- Miss McBoob got confused and began moving the pieces backwards.
- Clio tried to eat half the money.

- Declan fell asleep *on* the board and his tail kept flicking my hotels onto the floor.

And Liam basically made up his own rules and started haggling down prices. I'm sure he stole money from the bank and, well, um, I may have punched him on the nose. I don't know if the blood splatters will ever come off the notes.

'Oh boys,' Miss McBoob sighed. 'You two really need to learn how to get on. I would do anything to have a chance at rekindling my relationship with my brother.'

I zoned out. I'd heard this lecture about 4,444 times. In fact, every time she ever came over.

I perked up a little as I sensed Miss McBoob had *eventually* got to the end of her lecture and she started pulling things out of her gigantic handbag. Random wires and control pads fell out and a weird little metal top hat, but she quickly stuffed them all back in once she'd found what she was looking for. She proudly held out a crazy-looking, homemade laptop.

'Well, your mother said *no screen time* ... I made this baby with my new 3D printer, using carbon-based liquid crystals. I don't remember *them* being banned. How about some telly?'

'Can we watch something spooky?' Liam grinned, showing all his yellow teeth. (His creepy grin is THE MOST annoying thing in the world and he does it just to wind me up.)

'I want a thriller,' I moaned.

'Right ... Well, Clio, Declan and I are going to watch *A Detailed History into Backward Chaining Algorithms*. I've got a new project to research. Take it or leave it,' Miss McBoob shrugged, hoisting Clio onto her lap and throwing an ancient-looking blanket over them both. Dec leapt on top of them and spread himself into his favourite snoozing position. (Basically, any position.)

With nothing else to do, I stared, comatose as sciencey

people in lab coats droned on and on about I don't know what.

A triple, snorty sort of symphony came from the sofa and I glanced over. Miss McBoob, Clio and (predictably) Dec were all totally conked out, mouths gaping open and snoring loudly. I rolled my eyes and turned back to the never-ending documentary.

Hang on, I thought, spinning my head around again. *Where is Liam?*

LEVEL TWO

iam jumped guiltily as I hissed, 'Caught you!' He was perched on the loo with the door half open.

'Whose is that?' I yelled, seizing a futuristic-looking smartphone from his hands. 'Have you stolen Miss McBoob's phone? What were you thinking?'

'It's all good!' he said, grinning. (See, I told you). It definitely wasn't. I had plans. Computer gaming plans. When Mum came home, I needed her NOT to be cross so she'd lift the screen time ban.

I began to march the phone back to the living room

when Liam grabbed my arm.

'Wait, Max, there's something you have to see,' he exclaimed, pulling the phone from me and tapping on an app.

'How did you know the password?' I demanded.

'I used face ID, I only had to wave it in front of her snoozing schnozz and it unlocked,' he whispered. I swear, my brother is going to end up in prison one day.

'Just take a look at this,' he said, pulling me into our bedroom, and despite myself I couldn't quite resist the bubbling excitement in his voice. I yanked the phone off him and stared at a dull-looking game on the screen.

It was **so** basic. Just a pixilated room with clunky, rectangular furniture. Two tiny avatars (that looked a little like us) hopped about, and as far as I could work out you had to jump around trying to find certain objects.

'Er, this games looks *trash*. It must be about fifty years old,' I complained, confused why Liam was interested in it.

'But Max, can't you see …?'

'What, the lame graphics?' I snorted.

'It's *our* house! Look! There's the yellow sofa, the stripy blanket, the tiger cushion … it's our living room! Even that stain where you …'

I glared at him. **The Stain** was not to be mentioned. It may have been from a toilet-related incident that happened when I was very, very young.

'It's our house! Everything is in exactly the right place. The avatars … it's you and me!'

I shook my head at the stupidity of my brother but glanced again at the game. It was in demo mode and I watched the mini characters move automatically about the space. I had to admit, it was *slightly* amusing how much the layout seemed to mimic our flat.

In fact … the bedroom was almost an exact copy of ours … right down to the minute detail of the pile of dirty socks on Liam's side of the room. I looked, confused, from the phone to real life. Somehow my perfectly organized Pop Figures on my desk were in the same order.

'This is a bit weird,' I said, as a chill crept down my spine.

A pixelated cat suddenly popped up on the screen. Bizarrely, even this character looked a little bit like Dec: white with ginger paws and a tear in its right ear. Although *this* cat was creepy, with a purple top hat, waistcoat and evil-looking eyes. I shuddered.

'Welcome to Shrinkle! Are you ready to accept my challenge? One or two players?' the cat purred, sinisterly.

'Um … We should put the phone back before Miss McBoob wakes up,' I stammered.

'Oh, come on, just one go,' Liam urged, pulling the phone from my hands. He selected two-player and hit play.

'No, Liam!' I said, snatching the phone back off him. (I needed to complete that battle royal game I'd downloaded and I was *not* prepared to risk a weekend gaming ban on some dopey obby app or whatever this was.)

He tried to tear the phone out of my hands but it slipped from his grasp and spun high up into the air. *The phone's going to get broken*, I thought as it tumbled down. *That's it. We'll get punished for a month now …* I dived (like a world-class goalie) across the room to catch it, holding my breath.

Liam must have had the same thought as me. As the phone hit the hard ground millimetres from my outstretched fingers, my head crunched painfully with his. All I can really remember of what happened next was:

- a blinding rainbow light bursting out of the screen
- slamming my eyes shut and feeling a totally weird sensation all over, like I was somehow compacting into myself
- crash landing onto the floor.

'This is ALL your fault, Liam,' I shouted. The room was silent. I peeked open one eye.

If Liam runs back to the living room to pretend he's been watching the documentary and is going to try and lay the blame of a cracked screen — or worse — on me, I thought, *he should think again.*

'Liam?' I said, blinking. I looked around. The room had … *er* … changed.

Somehow the walls were now huge slabs of red, yellow and blue.

I spun around, dazzled. What was going on? I looked down. The floor was green and bumpy. *Where are the wooden floorboards? My spotty rug?* I crouched down and ran my fingers over raised letter shapes. It felt … plastic.

'L … E … G … O …' I read out, totally confused. I held my head in my hands.

Where is Liam? My heart began to thump anxiously in my chest, like a caged gorilla who wanted to escape.

'Helllooo?' I called out softly.

'This is **awesome**!' Liam shouted, as he jumped out from behind a huge, solid red rectangle as large as a table.

'W … w … where are we?' I stuttered, weakly.

'I don't know,' he grinned. 'But it's cool!'

'Oh, okay, this is just a dream,' I realized, suddenly laughing. 'Of course. I'm asleep in my bed and any minute I'll wake up and— *Ow!* Why did you do that?' I gasped as Liam pinched my arm.

'To see if you were sleeping,' he grinned. 'Or if we're in VR.'

'What do you mean, VR?' I asked.

'The game, Shrinkle! Maybe it's got a virtual reality setting?' he suggested. 'I don't know … One second I pressed play, the next minute, here we are.'

What is he talking about? How could we be IN the game? I looked up, searching for answers.

'Liam, does that look like our bedroom light to you

… but *much* further away than it should be? How can our ceiling be the same but the walls have changed? I don't like this. I want to go home,' I whimpered.

'Mmm, maybe we are home,' Liam said, slowly stroking the plastic walls. 'Do you know what I think, Max? We've shrunk and we're inside the LEGO castle you made about three years ago and refused to ever dismantle. Look! There's the little banquet table, the plastic goblets …' He pulled one off the table and pretended to take a sip. 'Ugh, dusty! Max, we've turned into LEGO figures!'

He was right. It was all surreally familiar, but we were the **wrong size**.

I closed my eyes again. *This cannot be real*, I thought. *Although … that pinch is still throbbing …* I could feel myself beginning to hyperventilate.

'Are you okay?' Liam asked.

'No, of course I'm not okay!'

'It's all good!' he said, grinning.

I tried to calm down and remember what I'd been taught at school — *just concentrate on breathing slowly.* It helped. *What should I do?* I thought. *Come on brain, don't freeze on me.*

I had three options to choose from:

1. panic — and yell my head off
2. really panic — roll into a ball and yell my head off
3. do something, anything … to try and turn things back to normal.

'If I can turn off the phone then whatever weird stuff is happening will just go away and we'll return to our proper size,' I stated, shakily, trying to suppress the instinct to just freak out.

I was sure it had landed somewhere near Liam's bed. If this really was the LEGO construction I'd made when I was seven, then we were in the corner of my room and the phone was only a metre or so away.

I looked up at the smooth walls. They were at least three times taller than me. I tried scaling them but I just slipped back down — there was nowhere to get a grip.

'Let's bash the wall down,' Liam grinned. He punched a blue rectangle, hard.

'Ouch!' he exclaimed, shaking his fist. The wall looked as sturdy as ever.

I needed a plan, but I couldn't think straight. If only we *were* in a game, then I'd know what to do.

'I need a pick axe!' Liam beamed, looking around.

'We are not in Minecraft,' I growled. Then suddenly it struck me. 'That's it. What if we *were* in Minecraft? We would build a staircase! Come on!' I attempted to heave the banquet table loose from the green base.

'It'd be easier to just break through,' Liam argued and he energetically began hitting a massive red brick.

'You are so annoying. I don't know how you've done it this time, Liam, but we are in this mess because of your irresponsible behaviour.' (*Wow*, I really sounded like Mum.) 'I … HATE YOU,' I spat (that was less Mum-like).

I pulled with all my might at the banquet block. It suddenly became loose.

'Ha!' I shouted, dragging it over to one of the walls. I ran over to where another block was fixed to the ground, vaguely remembering I'd placed this one here all that time ago for a LEGO knight to sit on. I pulled hard at it. I was beginning to get the hang of it now and satisfyingly stuck it on top of the red one.

I spun around, searching for more building blocks. Liam had sweat dripping from his face and was still bashing the wall, making no impression whatsoever. I shook my head angrily and continued to stack the bricks. It was hard work, but looking up I figured I just needed to pile two or three more and I'd be able to clamber over the top of the wall.

'Er … Max,' Liam garbled, suddenly sounding scared.

'Oh, have you finally realized my idea was better than

yours?' I said, climbing back down to get another block.

'Max ...' he said again, quietly. 'Help.'

'Help YOU? You're wasting time and energy ...' I replied, looking at him.

He stood deathly still.

'What is it now?' I said, rolling my eyes. A look of pure terror had fallen across his face.

I glanced around, my own hands beginning to tremble, as I took in eight towering, bristly legs, a cluster of beady, black eyes (each as large as a bowling ball) staring at us, and two, giant, razor-sharp fangs, oozing with venom.

A spider **the size of a cow** was standing in my LEGO castle.

'Don't move,' I whispered.

'Like, I'm going to move ...' Liam whimpered through gritted teeth. 'Max, it's going to eat me ...'

LEVEL THREE

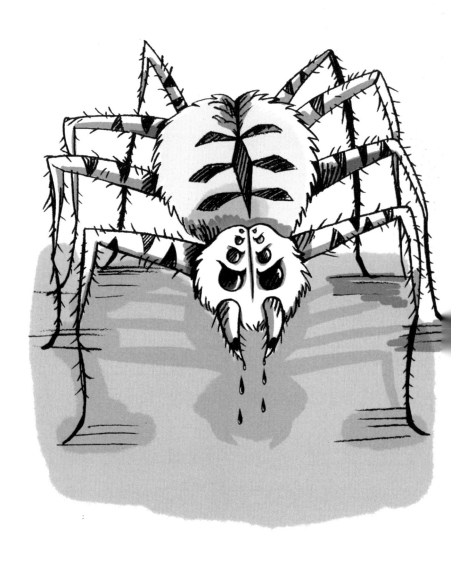

FRIDAY AFTERNOON, 4.43 P.M.
COUNTDOWN TIMER: 77 MINUTES

t that moment, I understood why Liam was scared of spiders. Spiders are TOTALLY terrifying close up (and magnified about ten thousand times). I'd never really looked at them before, having always been more amused by watching Liam howl like a baby when he came across one in the bath.

Wasps are *my* sworn enemy. And here's why:

- They ruin picnics.
- Unlike bees, who sacrifice their life for an attack,

wasps sting *as many times* as they want.

- Some wasps actually cram their eggs into their victims (okay, not humans, but cute insects like caterpillars). When the baby wasps hatch, they **eat their way out**. My baby sister can be pretty disgusting and I've seen her try to eat most things but she's definitely never done that.

- Once, when I was about six, a wasp actually flew into my mouth and I accidentally swallowed it. I was terrified that my own poo might sting me for weeks afterwards.

So, anyway, there I was. In my own LEGO trap, gawking at the truly hideous creature facing us. My palms were cold and sweaty and all I could think was: *I wish I was playing on my PC, nibbling a ketchup sandwich right now.*

'Max, please do something,' Liam mouthed. He was actually asking *me* for help.

I had to act. And fast.

I glanced up at the LEGO staircase and then at the alien-looking beast.

Just imagine you're in a computer game, I told myself.

Under my breath, I whispered, 'At the count of three, we're going to run up the stairs and I'll push you onto the top of the wall. Then you can pull me up and we'll jump down the other side. Okay?'

I didn't wait for a response.

'One … two …' *Will this work?*

'I can't move.' Liam gulped.

The spider suddenly jerked a huge leg forward and I screamed, '**Thrrreeeee!**'

I pulled Liam's hand and we clambered messily up the slippery steps.

'Don't look back,' I cried, and finding some sort of super-human strength I didn't know I had, I thrust my brother up.

Liam frantically grabbed the ledge. His foot squashed painfully down on my nose and I could almost taste the cheesy smell leaking from his socks.

'Your hand!' he yelled.

I threw my arm up, grasping his fingers, and tried to lever myself up. I flipped my right leg over the top, and before I could work out what to do next, we had both tumbled down the other side, landing in a heap on hard, wooden floorboards.

Scrambling up, we ran wildly and headed for cover. We reached a soft, fabric mountain and flopped behind it, gasping for breath. Too late, I realized it was a colossal pile of Liam's dirty washing, mostly consisting of smelly socks. At least we'd got away from the giant spider.

My heartbeat began to slow down and I let myself exhale.

'We did it!' Liam grinned. 'I thought we were gonners!'

I glared at him, stunned at his bravado.

'Liam, we're about seven centimetres tall. Spiders the size of TANKS could be looming around any corner. Imagine if a wasp comes along!?' My voice was getting so high pitched by this point that even I couldn't tell what I was saying.

I need to focus on getting to the phone, then this will all be over, I reminded myself. I scanned the vast room for it, now bigger than an Olympic stadium. A red light glowed from under Liam's bed. My heart sank.

You could describe Liam as messy. But that would be a compliment. It's more like he's completely disgusting and utterly disorganized.

My side of the bedroom is neat. Everything has a home.

My clothes hang in the wardrobe.

My books are in alphabetical order.

My spotty socks are all carefully matched.

My pants are in … actually you probably don't want to hear any more about my pants.

Every now and then, Mum shouts, 'Tidy your room!' and Liam shoves just about everything *and anything* under his bed and gets on with whatever he was doing.

It's bulging with half-sucked apple cores, damp, rotting football kits and snotty tissues. There *could* be treasure under there, no one would ever know and anyway, it would be covered in mould.

How could the phone have slipped under his bed? COULD THINGS GET ANY WORSE?

I quickly took back this thought, knowing quite well that, yes, yes they could, and I did NOT want to tempt fate. *The spider is probably licking its fangs and laying out the cutlery for a two-course feast at this very moment.*

'We need go under your bed,' I said. 'Right now, before the spider finds us.' (I'm not normally this decisive. Last week I spent so long in a sandwich shop trying to choose a filling, the shop closed for the day before I'd made up my mind.)

I felt a little bit of proud of myself. I'd got us away from the spider and now I was going to get us out of this nightmare.

But looking at Liam, I started to doubt my own

confidence. Liam (who never questions anything and just dives into disasters without a second thought) actually looked nervous. I guess he knew more than anyone what he'd crammed under his bed.

I began to feel sick to my bones as we jogged heavily towards the gloomy cave that was the terrifying no-man's-land of *under Liam's bed.*

It was more than freaky to be in such a familiar place but to experience it from such a different perspective. My desk was now **four storeys high** and the bookcase looked like a skyscraper. We had to leap over discarded paper clips and scramble over old comics as big as classrooms. I foolishly ran over a Pokémon card (the size of a double bed) and skidded across its shiny surface.

Just keep pretending this is a game, I told myself.

'Hey!' Liam shouted, sounding excited. I stopped in my tracks as he heaved up an old, army style action-man toy who was now taller than us. 'I'd forgotten all about this little guy!' he grinned, wrenching giant plastic arms forwards.

'Hurry up!' I snarled, anxiously. This wasn't the time to get nostalgic.

'Wait! I can use his gun as a weapon, and his outfit — I might put it on! Then I'll be camouflaged!'

'Right — if you were in the jungle!' I huffed and continued to march ahead.

'Help me with the Velcro at the back,' Liam called after me, as he tugged on the action figure's suit. I reluctantly pressed down the fabric. (Sometimes it was just easier to do what Liam asked.) He triumphantly pulled on army boots and popped a plastic green beret on his head.

'Sorry, mate,' he whispered to the now butt-naked toy discarded on the floor. 'I'll give you back your uniform later.'

I shook my head. 'You look stupid,' I grumbled, but I had to admit (to myself) he actually looked quite cool. I kind of wanted to find one of *my* old toys now. I scanned the gigantic room for a pirate robot toy I used to play with for hours — before I'd discovered Pirate Quest: Skull Treasure on my PC. His little sword might make a good weapon (it was actually insanely sharp, I'd accidentally cut my own finger on it once) and I'd look pretty good in his silver fabric cape.

But pirate-guy was nowhere to be seen.

'We're getting off task,' I huffed, and hurried to the foot of Liam's bed. I stared into the darkness. The glow of the phone's red light illuminated mysterious shapes and I couldn't quite make out a clear pathway towards it. Liam tried to hold my hand but I shook it off.

'Do you remember when we helped Dad build this bed?' he asked, looking up at the enormous slats. I rolled my eyes and started walking forwards.

'Yes. Of course. It was a terrible day. He yelled at us the entire time and he wouldn't let me use the electric screwdriver. And that was because *you'd* started messing

around with it, pretending it was your robot arm and then you dropped it, and—'

I stumbled and tripped over.

I felt around me and could just make out the dent in the floorboards that the electric screwdriver had created when it landed all that time ago. But now the dent was an enormous cavity.

'Come on, let's go this way,' Liam urged, hauling me to my feet.

It was getting darker as we moved slowly forward.

I groped nervously about for obstacles, a yucky film of dust caking my fingers. My foot tripped over enormous sheets of paper and I realized it was the IKEA manual that had been spread out while we attempted to construct the bed. I felt as if I could still hear Dad's angry, barking voice as he realized we'd somehow made the entire bed back to front and we'd have to unscrew it all and then start all over again.

How do I always get muddled up in Liam's messes? I

thought angrily. *Doesn't Liam realize Dad probably left because HE was always causing trouble?*

The bed-making debacle must have been one of last weekends we'd all spent together.

My tummy tied itself into a tight knot remembering the night Dad disappeared for good. There had been a LOT of very loud shouting from the living room and Liam had fetched Clio from her cot. We'd sat in silence, squidged together on my bed. (This was very unusual. As you know by now, Liam is NEVER silent.) It was a bit like when we were younger and we'd sit out huge thunderstorms together. Eventually, the front door had slammed and I haven't seen Dad since. Liam and Clio go for a milkshake with him every Saturday afternoon, but there's no way I'd go with that deserter.

Suddenly the **smell** hit me like a brick wall. Instantly, my train of thought about Dad shattered and I was thrust back into reality.

Even Liam began to retch and I don't think I've *ever*

seen him be sick. (I once saw him being dared to eat a toenail burrito. And he did, without gagging. I know what you're thinking: how is it possible that we're related?)

'What — is — that?' I gasped, as I felt my foot sinking into something moist. (Sorry for using *that word*. 'Moist' is without a doubt the third most disgusting word in the world. And it should NEVER be associated with chocolate cake. Holding place number two is *bulbous*. You know I'm right. But, in first place for the grossest word ever is **phlegm**. I don't like the way it's spelt or the way it sounds and surely *nobody* likes what it actually describes.)

I yanked my leg back up but my sock was sucked into the quicksand-like mush I was now half-submerged in.

'Er … I think it might be that goat's cheese and beetroot burger Mum made,' Liam gulped.

'You shoved it under your bed?' I gasped. 'That was about three months ago!' (Mum had had a vegetarian

health-kick kind of period after Dad left. Thank good-
ness she quickly moved on to her current ice-cream
fuelled diet. The freezer was now constantly stocked
with Häagen-Dazs. Fact: ice cream was first made with
ambergris … which is another word for **whale vomit**.
Sorry, I don't know why you needed to know that.)

Liam nodded slowly, his eyes watering with the
stench.

'This is *all* your fault. You led us this way,' I snarled
through gritted teeth. I clambered out of the decomposing bun, now barefoot and with lumps of mouldy beetroot dangling from between my toes.

'Ooh, look, I've found a coin!' Liam said gleefully. I
mean … seriously! *What possible use is a coin as big as a
wheel going to be to us RIGHT NOW?*

I twisted in a new direction and marched angrily
away from my brother.

'I'd be better off without you!' I shouted.

Then suddenly, I found I could no longer move.

Strange, sticky ropes seemed to pull at my body from every angle, and the more I struggled to get free the more I realized I was totally stuck.

'LIAM, HELP!' I shrieked, as his silhouette disappeared into the gloom.

'I've almost reached the phone,' Liam yelled back.

I squinted at the strange, unbreakable material that was imprisoning me. Then I was plunged into complete darkness.

'Max! The light on the phone's gone out!' Liam's voice called out.

'I can't move, Liam,' I screeched, wrestling to pull myself free.

'Where are you? Where's the phone? I can't see anything!' he called back.

'I'm trapped. I think it's a …' I didn't want to say it out loud, but I was pretty sure that THIS was the spider's lair and I had been captured in its web.

LEVEL FOUR

FRIDAY AFTERNOON, 4.53 P.M.
COUNTDOWN TIMER: 66 MINUTES

y heart was beating so loudly I was sure the spider would hear it. (What did spider ears even look like?)

I was totally helpless … my entire body was bound by spiderwebs as strong as chains. (Spider silk is so tough, it can be used to drag an aeroplane along! I know this because I'm always looking up spider facts to freak out my brother with.)

There was no way out. I was going to be **eaten alive**. (In fact, spiders don't eat, they suck the juices out of their prey … actually, that sounds way worse. *Maybe I should stop researching spiders.*)

I felt hot breath on the back of my neck. *This is it, this is really it,* I panicked, when I heard Liam's voice yell, 'Hiyah!'

I peered into the darkness. He was hacking away at the web with the action figure's gun!

'Take that!' he bellowed, until at last I felt the syrupy ropes fall down at my feet. I lunged forward … I was free!

'Liam, you did it!' I called out, groping for him. Then the hard plastic gun walloped me right on the nose. 'Ow! You can stop swinging that thing, I'm not trapped anymore,' I yelled, rubbing my poor schnozz.

'Oh, okay. Come on,' he said and I felt the comforting weight of his hand on my shoulder. I didn't shrug him off this time. We stumbled forward together, feeling nervously for the phone.

'Here it is,' I cried, as my hand struck smooth glass

that could only be Miss McBoob's phone. I felt for the round 'on' button, and pressed down hard, but nothing happened.

'Why is it dead, and we're still small?' I gasped.

'Let's pull the phone out from under the bed,' Liam suggested. So, without having a better idea, we hauled its mammoth weight towards the light.

It felt as if we'd burst outside as we finally reached the foot of Liam's bed. Totally shattered, I collapsed onto the ground. The relief at being able to see clearly again was overwhelming, and for a second I forgot that we were still smaller than pots of yoghurt.

I looked down, realizing I was covered from head to foot in cobwebs. Liam had saved me. *And* he hadn't started gloating about it yet.

'What now? How do we charge it?' Liam asked.

I looked at him in disbelief, feeling frustration and anger bubble up again inside me.

'How would I know?' I snapped. 'You got us into this

mess. And by the way, I'm never going to forgive you for the pants.' (That just slipped out. I hadn't meant to say anything about the PANTS. I felt mad with myself.)

'What pants?' Liam said, looking all innocent. My cheeks began to burn with rage.

Quickly changing the subject, I snarled, 'The phone is so heavy, dragging it even twenty centimetres was almost impossible.'

'Okay, okay, don't lose your temper. It's all good!' he said.

Just as a head's up, that is NOT what you should say to someone about to blow their top. Things like, 'Calm down, chill out, it's not that bad' have the opposite effect when I'm losing it.

I was about to launch myself at Liam when he suddenly shouted, 'Eureka!' in such a confident way I somehow overrode my instinct to jump on top of him.

Liam was pointing straight ahead. His old remote-control car lay abandoned and upside down, in front of us.

I don't think either of us had bothered playing with it for years. I remembered the Christmas he'd unwrapped it. I'd been *so* jealous because Liam was infuriatingly much better at driving it than me. I'd spent the rest of Christmas sulking in my bedroom after being punished for throwing mince pies at him. (The mince pies, it turned out, had been made by Miss McBoob and were stuffed with actual minced beef and not the fruity stuff you're meant to find in them. I had made quite a disgusting mess.)

'How can that help?' I asked, dumbfounded.

'Well, Mum's got a phone charger in her room — it looks like it might be the right size. We could whizz it straight to it!'

'How are we going to get the phone to stay on the car?' I huffed, but Liam galloped round to one of his bed posts and rolled out possibly THE MOST disgusting thing I have ever seen.

- MORE disgusting than Roman toothpaste, which was made from powdered mouse brains.
- MORE disgusting than discovering a baby toad in a can of lemonade. (Fred Davies, a boy in my class, said this happened to him last summer.)
- AND MORE disgusting than the fact that we all have tiny insects living on our eyelashes. If you don't believe me, Google it.

Anyway, you get the idea. This was gross. Really gross.

Liam, with a proud grin plastered on his face, was pushing a huge ball (bigger than him) towards me. It was pink, hairy and I swear there was a tooth sticking out of it.

'What is that?' I asked slowly.

'It's my gum ball. I call it Brenda. I've been working on it for years! I didn't want to show you until it was perfect, but ...'

'Working on it?' I asked, mystified.

'Every time I finish chewing gum, I add it to this

baby. I was hoping to break a record eventually, for the **world's biggest ball of gum**. But I'm prepared to sacrifice a lump or two to stick the phone down …'

My mouth hung open as I watched Liam pull four chunks off Brenda and stick them decisively to the corners of Miss McBoob's phone.

Without having the ability to think of anything else to say or do, I helped him flip the car over and we heaved the phone onto it. Liam clambered on top and by jiggling his bottom around, he squashed the phone firmly into place. I had to admit, it looked pretty stable.

Liam jogged over to where the dusty remote control lay. By some fluke, the batteries still seemed to be working.

'Right, you climb on and I'll steer from here. Then I'll catch you up and we can get the phone powered up.'

'I'm the eldest, I should steer,' I said indignantly.

'Max, you know I'm better at this,' Liam said smugly.

'But it's *my* turn,' I shouted, grabbing the huge control

pad off him. I pushed the joystick forward and the car shot off and crashed into the wall.

Huffing, I grumpily dropped the controller and climbed on top of the car.

If I'd had any minced-meat-mince pies to throw, I probably would have, but instead I held on and waited for the car to move.

Whoooosshhhh! I sped forward at what felt like one thousand miles per hour. My knuckles went white with the effort of holding on tight as I swerved round the door frame and shot like a bullet into Mum's room.

It was like playing a virtual reality racing car game but WITHOUT a steering wheel.

'**Stttoooppp thhhe caaaarrrr!**' I screamed as loud as I could, as the car rocketed towards Mum's bookcase. Just in time, it skidded to a halt but I was tossed forward, smashing my shoulder into Mum's giant bedside table.

'Owww,' I cried, rubbing my arm. I waited for Liam to run in after me so I could shout at him. But he didn't.

Eventually I grumpily heaved the phone off the car on my own and pushed Mum's huge charger into the hole. It fitted! I looked around again for Liam. What was he playing at?

I stared at the screen, waiting for a symbol to appear to signify power. A smiley face icon popped up on the screen. *Phew, at last we could sort this out!*

But why hadn't Liam followed me yet? Mum's room is literally next to ours. I suddenly became nervous the colossal spider might have discovered its web destroyed, tracked down my brother and was now getting its revenge. Nervously I crept back towards the hall. Mum's bedroom carpet was thick and it was a bit like moving through soft, long grass.

'Liam,' I called out, as my tummy began to fill with butterflies. 'Where are you?'

Suddenly, a towering **monster** thudded towards me. Huge crashing feet as big as trucks stomped along the hallway.

Compared to us, my baby sister was now taller than a block of flats. I threw myself against the skirting board to avoid her stampede as she bounded towards her bedroom. Huge globules of drool plunged down after her and I rolled myself tightly into a ball, terrified.

It was only when I heard the shriek of Liam calling out my name that I realized Clio was grasping my brother in her pudgy fist.

I breathed out slowly. This was a LEVEL TEN disaster. Utterly horrified, I ran after them, watching in dismay as Clio clumsily stuffed Liam into the little wooden bed in the top room of her doll's house and plonked a cover over him.

'Sleepy, sleepy,' she bellowed, still dribbling cascades of saliva.

Liam looked totally traumatized and he pulled the covers tightly up to his neck.

I'm going to have to rescue him, I realized. *But how?*

FRIDAY AFTERNOON, 4.57 P.M.

COUNTDOWN TIMER: 62 MINUTES

 frantically waved my arms and yelled, 'Clio!' to get her attention. 'You have to put Liam back on the floor. *Carefully.*'

Clio turned her enormous head slowly and looked at me, her eyes bright with interest. I felt like I was dealing with a Tyrannosaurus rex straight out of a Jurassic World film, and not my chubby two-year-old sister.

'No. Naughty Clio. Put me down,' I cried with as

much authority as I could manage as my Godzilla-sister enveloped me in her grasp.

I found myself flung painfully into the doll's bed next to Liam, and Clio's gigantic, snot-smeared face peered at us with fascination. Her nostrils, the size of bathtubs, breathed heavily on me and I began to tremble with fear.

'Nighty nighty, lil' Maxy,' she cooed, prodding the cover with her enormous finger.

'How did … Why did … What …?' I stuttered at Liam, as Clio began to sing 'Winkle, winkle, pickle star …' at an unbelievably loud volume. The doll's house curtains actually shook with the noise, and huge cannon-balls of saliva projected out of her mouth.

'Just pretend you're asleep,' Liam hissed, and we both slammed our eyes shut and prayed Clio would leave us alone.

'Ga-morning!' she boomed and whipped the cover away, tossing it behind her back. Liam and I clung to each other, feeling ridiculously vulnerable and helpless.

'Clio, we're … fragile, be careful,' I cried as she grabbed the bed and flew it above her head, swooshing it around like a toy aeroplane. Liam and I clasped the slippery wooden edges in desperation.

'Make this stoooopppppp!' I cried, as Clio began to sing 'Zoom, zoom, zoom, we go-in to da moon'.

She stomped heavily around the room. I was suddenly thrust off the bed and flung forwards, spinning through the air. Time seemed to go into slow motion, as I watched Liam lose his grip too and rocket towards me. *This really is the end,* I thought. In my favourite video game, a parachute would appear magically on your back in a situation like this. But we were free falling from a preposterous height and were about to slam into the rock hard floor.

Splllaaatttt!

Amazed, I realized something incredibly soft and squidgy had broken my fall. I was alive!

Liam howled in pain as he crashed next to me, then

looked up confused, wiping his eyes. Strange brown smears ran down his face, and it was then I understood: we had landed in **Clio's nappy bin**.

We gagged at the smell and I scrambled to get out. But Liam, with lumps of poo between his fingers, pulled me back down into the soiled pile of nappies.

'Shhh,' he whispered, pointing at Clio, who we could still see bombing around the room searching for us. I ducked my head down and clamped my hand tightly over my nose to try and keep out the smell from wafting in, as she called out, 'Tiny Maxy … Lil' Liam? Where are oo?'

Eventually Clio careered out into the hallway to look for us and I pulled myself out of the nappy bin. I ran to where Mum kept the baby wipes and rubbed at my skin and clothes to desperately try and get the smears and stench off.

'Liam? You okay?' I asked, as he hobbled slowly over to me. He'd lost his army beret and was propping himself along with the stump of a pencil.

'I think I must have twisted my ankle when I landed,' he said, rubbing his foot.

'It's all good. It just … hurts when I walk. So what happened with the phone?' he asked, scraping lumps of our sister's nappy contents off his cheek.

'The phone! It turned on!' I cried, remembering the smiley face icon. *I could be having a normal-size, hot shower in an instant.* 'It's charged … What are we waiting for?' I said, and I bolted back towards Mum's room.

Reassuringly, I could hear Clio bellowing a nursery rhyme in the kitchen.

Panting for breath, I reached Miss McBoob's phone and tapped on the creepy Shrinkle app icon.

Liam eventually limped up next to me.

'There MUST be a way to end the game,' I said, swiping through images.

The sinister, pixelated white cat appeared, licking his lips. His face was now bigger than ours.

'So, are you ready to begin?' the phone asked out loud.

'No, we don't want to play!' I yelled. 'Make us big again.'

I tried pressing buttons and clicking anything possible. I stamped the phone's 'on' button and even switched the whole thing off and on again. But nothing happened.

We were still only seven centimetres tall!

'So, are you ready to begin?' Shrinkle's cat repeated. I looked at Liam in anguish.

'What are we going to do?' I asked.

'I guess we have to play the game,' he replied, and there was a tiny curl in the corner of his mouth.

'Are you smiling? Are you finding this *fun*?' I stammered.

'No, I mean, well, it's quite exciting isn't it!' he said, grinning openly now.

I bit my bottom lip in disbelief. We had almost been:

- devoured by a spider
- swallowed up by quicksand-like beetroot mush

- and worst of all, been suffocated by Clio's nap-pies.

'Which bit of this is exciting?' I bleated, exasperated.

'What flies without wings?' the cat suddenly asked in a trill, and I spun round to look at the phone.

'What?' I asked, confused.

'I know! It's "time"!' Liam grinned, looking pleased with himself. 'Time flies … when you're having fun …' he trailed off.

I think Liam could tell I was beginning to lose my temper in a BIG WAY.

'Time! Ha ha, well done,' the cat purred. 'Your countdown timer has now begun.' An image of an egg timer popped up on the screen, trickling a thin stream of sand from the top to the bottom.

'You have precisely one hour to solve my three riddles, find the objects and beat me! Easy peasy. Good luck!' the pixel cat laughed, menacingly.

'One hour?' I cried. 'One hour — then what? What if we don't solve the riddles … or find the objects. What will happen to us …?'

A cold, clammy sweat sprang up all over my body and my heart began to pump at turbo speed.

'Don't worry, Max, I'm good at riddles,' Liam smiled confidently, like our lives were not at stake.

'*Rrrr* … riddle one,' the cat said, rolling the 'r' with delight.

'Find: the only place in the world where today comes before yesterday.'

'What?' I stuttered. 'I don't understand what that even means. Today comes *after* yesterday, and *before* tomorrow.'

'We've got to think outside the box,' Liam suggested.

'What box? I've been in a nappy, but no box … yet.' I put my head in my hands.

'Concentrate on the riddle,' Liam said, sitting in a yoga position with a constipated look on his face.

The phone made a tick-tock sound and I started to run

in a circle like a deranged puppy.

'Today before yesterday … Argh, what does that mean?'

Then, like a bowl of ice cream had been tipped over my head, the answer hit me. I'd spent my entire Friday afternoon at school (before the pants disaster) having to rearrange boring words into the correct alphabetical order …

The only place you can find Today before Yesterday was IN THE DICTIONARY!

'That's it! Dictionary!' I shrieked with joy. The cat was motionless on the screen.

'T comes before Y in a dictionary. I worked it out!' I yelped. 'Why aren't we on to riddle two?'

'The cat said we've got to find the object,' Liam said. 'Mum must have a dictionary somewhere.'

We both stared up at Mum's looming bookcase, stuffed with ornaments, old bits of clutter, a coin jar and maybe, just maybe, a dictionary.

'I don't think I can climb with my bad leg,' Liam sighed, sounding disappointed.

Suddenly full of determined energy, I ran to the lumps of chewing gum that were gluing the phone to the remote control car and yanked off four pieces.

'I'll go,' I said, feeling a bit like the hero of a game.

Without trying to overanalyze if I was doing the right thing, I started scaling the wall, using the sticky balls of Brenda to heave myself up to the books.

Don't look down, don't look down, I repeated to myself, anxiously scanning the titles. Some of these must have been Dad's old books. He had a weird taste in historical romance that he used to attempt (but failed) to get me interested in. I tried to ignore them and the fact my Mum had a stack of books with titles like:

- *Sibling Rivalry: How to encourage your children to be friends*
- *Nightmare Children: How to cope*
- *The Explosive Child: Top tips*

Was I really that bad?

'Look Max, there's a book called *Girl on a Budget* and it's by someone called Penny Pincher!' Liam shouted up.

I rolled my eyes and continued to search for a dictionary.

It was clear I did not get my neat gene from Mum. I hate to admit I'm anything like Dad, but he was always tidier than Mum when he lived here. Her books were back to front, upside down and *not even* colour coded.

I stumbled past some enormous photos that were sticking out from between two notebooks. One was of Mum, Dad and me, and must have been taken when I was really little. I guess it was Halloween. We were all dressed as pumpkins and sat in descending size order. Dad was laughing. He never laughed. In fact, we all looked happy. I cranked my head to one side to look at the next photo. There was baby Liam in my lap, looking like a wrinkled prune. Dad was sitting next to me, his face tired and stressed. I knew it. Everything had started to go downhill in this family when my brother came along.

'Go up a level,' Liam yelled. 'There's a little yellow book, one floor up, I think it's a dictionary …'

I pressed the pink gum onto the wall and suckered myself even higher. The Brenda balls were beginning to lose their stickiness and I felt myself wobble a little. Without being able to stop myself, I looked over my shoulder to see how high I was. My head swam at the sight of my tiny brother and the ground far below and my tummy did a triple somersault. There was no nappy to soften my fall now.

I took a deep breath and kept going. At last, I reached the next row of books and pulled myself up on to the ledge. I had to clamber over a weird, creepy clown figurine covered in earrings, and as I pulled my leg back over it, the clown teetered on the edge then tumbled off the bookcase, spiralling through the air. The earrings flew off it like deadly torpedoes.

'**Watch out below**!' I bellowed, as they crashed around Liam. The clown struck the ground and shattered as if a grenade had been thrown.

'Liam!' I called out nervously, holding onto a book to steady myself as I peered down at the carnage.

From under the wreckage, Liam threw up his little hand in a thumbs-up position and I sighed with relief. I edged forward and finally reached a small yellow book. The spine clearly said DICTIONARY. I stretched my hand out and pressed it, firmly.

'I found it. Has the cat said anything?' I hollered.

'Mmm. Nothing. Maybe you have to say the name of the object?' Liam called up.

'Dictionary!' I said, fervently, pressing harder. I heard a chiming reward sound ring out and Liam whooped with joy.

'You did it,' he cheered, as I scrambled back down, relieved to feel the thick carpet envelop me as I reached the ground.

I ran to look at the phone and the screen showed a flashing, glittering crown. Liam wrapped himself around me and I couldn't help but beam with happiness.

'We make the best team!' he said. 'It's just like when we were little. Do you remember when we used to dress up like superheroes, with our pants over our trousers, and go on pretend missions round the flat?'

'Well, you'd know all about pants,' I spat, meaningfully.

'Huh? You're obsessed with pants today,' he replied, looking confused (with his excellent poker face).

I was about to leap on top of him when Shrinkle's cat purred, 'Congratulations players! Now for *Rrrr* … riddle two!' making us both jump.

LEVEL SIX

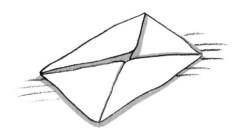

FRIDAY AFTEROON, 5.13 P.M.
COUNTDOWN TIMER: 44 MINUTES

n a sneering voice, Shrinkle's cat demanded, 'Now, my little players, I want you to find: what can't be used until it's broken.'

'I know what that is!' Liam cried and he hobbled decisively over to a pile of letters stuffed under Mum's bed.

'Envelope!' he shouted gleefully. But a horrible, 'Du-du-duuuuuhh,' sound belted out from the phone. I looked at the screen in horror as Shrinkle's cat wrinkled his nose and said, 'I'm afraid *that* was the incorrect answer. You have lost a life.'

'What?' I shouted in dismay. 'A life! But ...' I stared at Liam, who stood looking perplexed next to the bed. 'Why did you do that? We should have discussed it first. An envelope? That doesn't even make sense. Why don't you ever stop to think?'

'But I thought, you know, you have to open an envelope to use it. You break the paper ... I just ... I'm sorry, Max. I didn't mean to ...'

If he dares say 'It's all good!' I will not be held responsible for my actions.

I began to really panic. 'How many lives do we have? Can we win one back?'

I manically began searching through the game's menu pages to try to find answers. A colourful list titled 'stats' sprang up. I scanned the contents, frantically.

Strength: 48 out of 100

Endurance: 89 out of 100

Agility: 72 out of 100

Intelligence: 59 out of 100

And then below, in bold:

Riddles completed: 1 of 3

Lives: 2 (out of 3)

Time limit remaining: 41 minutes and 22 seconds

'But there are two of us,' I cried. 'Why is there only one stats page? We should each have stats, surely? And there are only *two* lives remaining. What happens if we lose all our lives? Liam, what have you done?'

Liam read the figures over my shoulder and shrugged. 'Perhaps there's only one stats page because the game combines both our skills ... and weaknesses. I guess, um, we're a team. We either win together ... or lose together.'

'Well, I don't want to be in your team,' I growled. 'I didn't ask for any of this. I don't want to play with you.'

'Hang on! I think I've worked out what the answer

might be. An egg!' Liam said, grinning. 'You have to *break* an egg to use it! There must be a box of them the kitchen.'

'I am not taking any more risks. This is stupid. And dangerous. I'm going to tell Miss McBoob. This is her phone, she must've downloaded the game. She'll be able to help.'

I turned determinedly towards the living room.

'Max, we should stick together. Remember what happened with Clio,' Liam said, in a pleading voice. I did remember, all too clearly. And I'd had enough.

'I can't run as fast as you — my leg ...' Liam yelled. But I didn't look back.

Stupid Liam and his stupid ideas and his stupid twisted ankle. Intelligence 59 out of 100. Hmph, I thought, angrily. How could that be right? *And strength. Only 48!* Those stats must be wrong.

Worryingly, I couldn't see or hear where Clio was, but I tried to stay focused. *Miss McBoob will help us,* I figured. I finally reached the living room and looked up at the now gargantuan yellow sofa. On it, our humongous, foil-covered neighbour was horizontal and snoring loudly.

Declan was nowhere to be seen. (Maybe he was actually awake … More likely he'd just found somewhere else to snooze.)

So what was the best method to wake up Miss McBoob?

- Pinch her?
- Do an impression of an alarm clock in her ear?
- Tickle her with a feather?
- Throw water at her face?

None of these seemed like great options, so I just focused on reaching her first.

I looked around for inspiration. In front of my eyes, the room transformed into a giant platform game. It wasn't that anything had actually changed, it's just that after years of perfecting my skills on these sort of computer games, I could instantly spot the best route to get to Miss McBoob. *Mum is constantly complaining about how much time I waste on my PC,* I thought, *but now all those hours might just save my life!*

I realized if I could scramble on top of the magazine rack, I'd be able to leap onto the footrest. From there, I might be able to climb up the coffee table leg, and then, using one of Mum's wooden flowers, I'd be able to vault myself onto Dad's leather reclining chair.

Why had Mum kept that chair? She should chuck it out. Or burn it. Dad was never coming back. You could still make out his bum cheek imprint on it. How could he have gone and left us, leaving a gaping Dad-shaped hole in our lives?

I don't know what Dad would think if he knew what I was up to right now, but I'm certain of this: he'd tell me I was doing it wrong. If I got 99 percent correct in a test, he'd want to know why I hadn't got 100 percent. Or

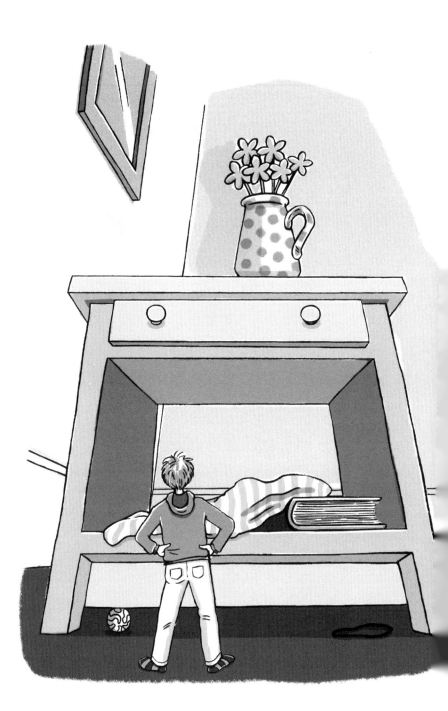

he'd tell me off for something Liam had done. Like when Liam tried to bake homemade chewing gum and he accidentally set fire to the kitchen. I got blamed for not stopping him. Or when we missed the flight to Spain last year because Liam got stuck in the airport toilets. (Okay, yes, I'd broken the toilet lock … but that's because Liam had wound me up so much.)

Nothing I did was ever good enough for my dad. Just once, I wish he could have said he was **proud** of me.

Shaking thoughts of Dad angrily out of my head and narrowing my eyes, I refocused.

From the chair, I just needed to swing across the curtains and I would land right next to Miss McBoob's face, and er … then wake her up somehow.

I just needed a hook to help me get across the curtains. And that's when I remembered Mum's fallen earrings! I raced back to her room.

Liam was gone. Just his little pencil walking stick lay discarded on the floor next to the phone. I grabbed a sharp, curved earring from the floor, pushed it through my belt and sprinted back to the living room.

Miss McBoob made a **huge snort**, which made me jump with fear, and I found myself worrying if Liam was okay.

'No, Max,' I told myself. 'Don't think about Liam.' *I am going to sort this out alone. I'm better off without my brother and his reckless decisions. He planted PANTS on me — in front of the ENTIRE class.*

I pulled myself onto Mum's towering pile of 'inspirational' magazines. I don't think I've actually ever seen Mum *read* any of these, but I swear she has subscriptions to:

- *Rugs Today: For all your rug needs*
- *The History of the Paper Clip*
- *The Cabbage Diet: 1000 ways to cook cabbage* (So that's where Mum had come up with the horrendous idea of cabbage lasagne!)

From there, I leapt onto the coffee table and using the wooden flower, sprang onto Dad's chair. Scrambling across, I threw myself forward and plunged Mum's earring deep into the curtain. My plan was working!

I rocked back and forth, creating momentum and then, counting down from

three …

two …

one … I thrust myself towards Miss McBoob.

LEVEL
SEVEN

FRIDAY AFTERNOON, 5.13 P.M.
COUNTDOWN TIMER: 28 MINUTES
LIVES: 2/3

 couldn't believe I'd actually pulled it off!

As I soared through the air, I laughed out loud at those ridiculous stats. It was *obviously* Liam dragging down our scores.

But too late, I realized I wasn't going to land on the spongy sofa. Or even on Miss McBoob's fuzzy face.

I was heading straight into Miss McBoob's **cavernous mouth**.

I clasped at the hairs of her wiry moustache but they slipped through my fingers and I plunged down, her gaping lips sliding past my hands. I grasped one of her saliva-soaked teeth, pleading with the universe that it wasn't false and wouldn't budge. Her wild tongue lashed about, sending spit bombs soaring at me and her tonsils darted around a hole that led to … her insides.

I was going to get **swallowed alive** by Miss McBoob.

'*Help*!' I called out pitifully.

It was only a matter of time and I would be joining those fourteen cups of tea and seventy-two miniature cupcakes she'd wolfed down during Monopoly. And no one would ever know what had happened to me. There was no computer game knowledge or skills I could apply to this situation.

Every time Miss McBoob snored out, I got caked in a moist film that soaked me down to my underwear. Every time Miss McBoob snored *in*, it was far, **far** worse.

My hand slipped a little further down her tooth and closer to her slimy, throbbing pink throat. (A tooth, it turns out, does not have a lot of grip.)

I tried to think of what my last words should be. (Apparently, Bob Hope, Dad's favourite comedian, said on his deathbed, 'Did you hear the one about the guy who died mid-sen—' which I think is pretty funny.)

I searched my brain for a joke that would be the crowning sentence of my life. 'What's a dog's favourite pizza …?' I asked wistfully.

'PUP-eroni …' Liam replied in a majestic sounding voice. I looked up disbelievingly, but there he was, dangling from Miss McBoob's nose!

'Liam!' I shouted gleefully, 'You found me! How?' I didn't even care that he'd ruined my joke, and potentially my final utterance on this Earth. He'd come to save me!

'Clio's baby monitor!' he grinned. 'I heard you crying and saying something about last words?'

I blushed bright red. 'Mmm. Get me out of here, Liam.'

He held out the plastic gun and I grabbed hold

of it, managing to get my foot onto Miss McBoob's cracked top lip. I swung my other arm upwards and grasped her quivering nostril hairs, then heaved myself up. She jerked her head and abruptly sneezed, **'Accchhhppssplewww!'**

We both torpedoed off her face along with several gallons of lumpy green snot. (For quite a petite and wrinkly person, she created an awful lot of nose slime.) We crashed, head over heels, into Mum's tiger cushion at the other end of the sofa.

I was now covered in rotten beetroot, cobwebs, nappy juice, saliva *and* old lady gunge … but … I WAS STILL ALIVE!

I looked at Liam. He was clutching his bad ankle, his face distorted in pain. I'd nearly lost everything … This felt like a second chance to make things up with my brother.

'Liam,' I muttered, feeling ashamed. 'I abandoned you and … you rescued me. I thought I was going to get

swallowed. Um … thank you.'

He looked at me earnestly and I think we both realized this was a momentous moment. I'd actually thanked him. (And not in a sarcastic 'Thanks *a lot* for ruining my life' way, but in a 'Thank you for being there for me' kind of way.)

Somehow, knowing he would risk everything for me, even after I'd totally deserted him, made me realize Liam wasn't my enemy. He was my brother. And we were in this together.

'Thanks, bro. Love you,' Liam said, blushing and grinning at the same time. 'Can I have your Golden Homer Simpson figure then?' he asked hopefully.

'As if,' I huffed, as we slid carefully onto the floor.

'Max, I do need your help with something …' Liam said awkwardly.

'Of course, anything …' I stuttered, and I meant it (within reason). I mean, he'd just saved my life.

'I need to do a poo.'

I looked at him in disgust.

'I can't go on the actual toilet … *obviously*. That would be really dangerous. What if I fell in and got flushed? I guess it'd be like careering down a turbo-charged, incredibly long and bendy water slide … And that would be awesome … but it would also be full of wee and poo and I might end up in a rat-infested sewer …' he trailed off.

'I don't know, just go in the corner,' I said, shrugging.

'I can't. I don't think I'll be able to go unless I'm ON a toilet. What am I going to do?'

'Hold it in then!' I said, shaking my head in disbelief that I was actually having this conversation.

'No, but I need to. It's uncomfortable …'

Avatars don't suddenly pop off to the toilet when they're obliterating aliens or escaping rampant tornadoes … I couldn't keep pretending I was in a game if I had to deal with my brother needing a **number two**.

'How about … Clio's doll's house toilet?' I suggested, half kidding.

'Yes! That's a brilliant idea,' he said, and so, unbelievably, we detoured to Clio's room.

I drummed impatiently on my leg, glancing at my watch every other second as I waited for Liam to reappear.

'Hang on, what's that?' I said, slowly, noticing a black backpack shoved down the side of the doll's house.

'What the …?' I began to stutter … It was my black backpack. My eyes wide in disbelief, I suddenly remembered — I had plonked it there last night while I was playing with Clio.

I must have taken Mum's identical backpack into school … full of her dirty washing loaded for the laundrette. (Our washing machine's been broken for three weeks.)

So Liam hadn't pranked me … He had nothing to do with the pants!

Okay, so Min still thought I was an underwear-collecting weirdo (and that was pretty bad), but at least

I didn't have to be mad with Liam anymore! I felt a huge surge of relief overtake me, like I'd had a tight ball of anxiety in my tummy that I'd now pooped out.

'I feel a lot better,' Liam grinned, clambering out of the doll's house and zipping up his pants.

'Me too!' I said, smiling.

'Liam …' I said, cringing a bit.

'Yup?' he replied.

'Love you too,' I mumbled.

'I know,' he said with a wink. 'Now for the egg! Come on, think about it. It's the right answer. What else could it be?'

'Okay,' I sighed, the plan to wake Miss McBoob having failed so dramatically. 'I hope you're right.'

I helped him limp to the kitchen and we looked up at the soaring, impenetrable fridge.

'How on earth are we going to get in?' I asked, despondently.

Liam started enthusiastically listing all kinds of

TERRIBLE ideas, like:
- hurtling me up to the fridge using the catapult toy he'd been given three birthdays ago
- firing me at the door on a suction-headed arrow
- strapping me to a drone and whizzing me to the handle.

Basically, he came up with lots of different ways to launch me at the fridge that wouldn't actually help us reach an egg in any way, as I'd still be on the wrong side of the door.

'Maybe we can touch a *head lice* egg in your hair?' I cried, the idea popping into my head in a proper cartoon-lightbulb moment.

'For the last time, I don't have nits,' he muttered. He did. I've seen him scratching his scalp LIKE MAD when he's asleep.

I hurled myself at his head and yelled, 'Egg!'

'Gerrofff,' Liam said, ducking, but I managed to slap his forehead.

'I'll run back to the phone and see if that worked and if Shrinkle's given us the final riddle,' I asserted, looking at his ankle, which by now was pretty swollen. 'You stay here. Just, um, hide behind the broom and don't get squashed or eaten or anything.'

I ran, panting, to Mum's bedroom and as I turned into the doorway, an earth-shattering wail rang out.

It was Clio. She'd climbed up Mum's chest of drawers and was now standing on top, wobbling and clearly unsure how to get down.

Clio has an impressive ability to get herself into stupidly dangerous situations.

Here are her top four (from the last two weeks):

1. I found her **stark naked** stuck down the loo last Friday.

2. On Monday, I caught her sharing a meal with Dec. And, just to be clear, I mean they were eating cat food together. She was on the floor

in Miss McBoob's flat, licking FISH FOOD CASSEROLE off her fingers.

3. At the weekend, she managed to get into the fridge and cover herself from head to foot in butter and then ran around like a greasy lunatic. It was almost impossible to catch her as she just slipped out of everyone's hands.

4. She peed on the floor in the changing rooms at the swimming pool. Okay, that wasn't exactly dangerous, but it was *so* embarrassing.

A giant baby sob splashed onto my head, instantly soaking me through.

I really didn't want Clio to spot me and decide to play doll's houses again, but I also didn't want the Worst Brother in the Universe Award for leaving her up there to fall and hurt herself.

'Oh Clio, be careful,' I cried, waving my arms about to get her attention. 'Clio, Clio, come down — slowly!' I shouted at the top of my voice.

At last she spotted me and stopped crying. 'Tiny Maxy!' she smiled.

'You come down here this instant!' I shouted, hoping she could hear me.

'Clio climb UP!' Clio cooed, proudly.

'Yes, you did. But now I need you to get down. Without falling.'

Amazingly, she turned around and clambered back down the drawers. And thankfully, she reached the ground in one piece. I charged to the phone, but the screen was still disappointingly displaying riddle number two. Touching the head lice eggs clearly hadn't worked.

I anxiously searched the stats. Now, there was only one life remaining. A chill travelled down my spine. One life? I started hyperventilating. We couldn't afford any more mistakes.

'Liddle Maxy okay?' my huge sister breathed hotly into my face.

'Um, Clio …' I said, trying to calm down and keeping just far away enough from her to be out of reach. 'Do you think you could you open the fridge again?'

Mum had put a baby lock on it after the butter incident, but I figured if Clio could lift me up I could flip the tricky latch, then she could do the heavy work of opening the door.

'Come on, Clio!' I called, running backwards towards to the kitchen, encouraging her to follow. Her heavy footsteps crashed terrifyingly close to my tiny body, but my plan was working.

'Max, are you mad? Why are you getting Clio to follow you?' Liam cried, peeking out from behind the broom as we reached the kitchen.

'I've got an idea,' I exclaimed, trying to focus on the moment. *I won't tell him about losing another life*, I thought. *It won't help.*

'Right. Clio, do you want to play with the butter again?'

Liam looked at me like I'd lost my mind. He'd been roped in to helping catch our slithery sister when she'd buttered herself like a piece of toast, and it really hadn't been pretty. We were still finding smears of butter in the most inappropriate places (on the toilet, up the walls, all over Mum's favourite blanket).

I explained (as clearly as I could to a giant baby), that I needed her to lift me up to the lock, and amazingly she understood. (I think I've been underestimating how much Clio gets, seeing as she can only say about twenty words and mainly cries and chucks food around when she isn't climbing up stuff.)

I still couldn't help but tremble with fear as she lifted me up to the latch.

'Gently,' I called out, my voice wobbling. 'That's my arm you're crushing, Clio,' (in your jumbo baby fist).

I heaved open the latch and Clio spared no time in yanking open the white fridge door. She shoved me onto a shelf and then began pulling out goodies for herself as fast as she could (obviously expecting to get stopped by a grown-up at any second). The floor was very quickly a puddle of jam, yoghurt and ham, all mulched together. Meanwhile, I jumped in and started to search frantically for anything egg box shaped.

It was freezing. My feet instantly felt like blocks of ice stuck to my legs. My breath came out in dragon smoke. My hands shook wildly with the cold and my body began to stiffen up. My movements were as creaky as a rusty robot.

'Where are the eggs? We always have eggs,' I stammered. (Even when things were really bad after Dad left and Mum spent days in bed, somehow there were ALWAYS eggs in the fridge. I perfected cooking scrambled eggs that week and that's basically all we ate for seven days.)

I hoisted myself up to another shelf. There were NO EGGS anywhere. *I need to solve this riddle,* I reasoned, *otherwise what will happen to us?* I looked at my fingers which ached with the cold and were already turning blue. I didn't know what to do.

Suddenly I remembered Mum preparing the party food last night. She had used dozens of eggs glazing all those tiny brioche buns for the big event. *There must be MOUNTAINS of eggshells in the bin,* I thought, feeling a mixture of relief and fear.

I would have to go in the bin.

FRIDAY AFTERNOON, 5.43 P.M.
COUNTDOWN TIMER: 14 MINUTES
LIVES: 1/3

 stiffly clambered out of the fridge and attempted to rub my body frantically up and down to get warm. I even let Liam squeeze me tight to get the feeling back into my limbs.

'I can't believe this is the day I'll witness my clean-freak brother climb INTO a bin!' he said, shaking his head and sniggering after I'd told him my new plan.

'I'm not a clean freak. I just believe in hygiene.'

(I'm not sure I've *ever* witnessed my brother having a

bath. I honestly think he believes going swimming every now and then counts for washing.)

'And what other options do we have?' I asked. 'I don't *want* to go in the bin. But there can only be about twenty minutes left and then what?'

'Well, at least we've still got two lives if "egg" isn't the right object,' Liam replied. He was trying to sound reassuring but instead I felt a sharp pang of guilt for not telling him about losing the second life.

Clio was distractedly playing with the jam–ham–yoghurt concoction and had now added to it with chicken legs and chocolate mousse. She had it smeared all over her face and a sheet of ham flapped from her nose.

I tried not to think about the revolting image or risk of salmonella as Liam and I tugged a shoelace out of my sneaker and I bravely tied it around my waist. Then I helped him clamber up the spice rack till we were both on a ledge just above the bin.

I realized we had never before spent so long in each

other's company without biting each other's heads off. I don't think I'd even punched him for at least forty minutes. That was probably a world record for us.

'Are you sure about this?' Liam asked, peering down into the mountain of rotting food. Brown banana peel lay limply over chewed bread crusts. Last night's curry mingled with discarded baked beans, and fish bones bulged with grey rice pudding.

I swallowed, nervously. I was about to experience my WORST nightmare.

But there were clearly heaps and heaps of eggshells. If Liam could just hold the shoelace steady and hover me above the bin, I would be able to reach out and touch a fragment of egg without actually going in.

I held my breath as Liam slowly lowered me down. I could hear him wheezing with the effort. *Why couldn't it have been my leg to get hurt?* I wished silently. Liam would have probably enjoyed this and pretended he was on a SWAT mission.

The hodgepodge of putrid food got closer and closer to my face. The stench wafted uncontrollably up my nostrils. But an eggshell thankfully lay on top of the pile of debris.

'Okay, Liam, just hold on tight,' I yelled, stretching out my arm, my fingers reaching out desperately for the shell. It was just out of my grasp. I strained forward. 'Egg, egg!' I shouted, trying to magically lengthen my stubby arm. I thrust myself forward, trying to swing the shoelace to get me just a tiny bit closer. 'Egg!' I said again, making contact AT LAST with the hard, creamy shell.

'You can stop now,' I yelled up to my brother.

'DROP now?' Liam called back down.

'No! Stop, STOP, not drop,' I cried as, too late, I felt the taught shoelace suddenly become loose and I plunged head first into the festering waste.

I slipped deeper and deeper, past every awful texture and smell you can imagine (or, understandably, you might choose not to). It was truly **horrible** and

seemed to go on forever.

Eventually, I managed to grip onto something hard ... some cardboard packaging perhaps. I had no idea, it was pitch black. This was worse, far worse, than being under Liam's bed.

Then I realized something was MOVING in the bin. I swallowed hard. *Please don't let there be maggots*, I thought, closing my eyes. Mum had woken me up screaming once when she'd found a black bin bag swarming with maggots. Apparently, if flies can get into food waste, they lay eggs that then hatch into squirming, chubby white maggots within twenty-four short hours.

Maggots are so gross, they make wasps seem bearable in comparison.

- If a maggot gets injured, the other maggots have a feeding frenzy on it ... that's proper evil cannibalism.
- I also found out (I got a little bit obsessed with

maggots after the bin bag incident) that they are actually used in some medical procedures to clear out wounds — by eating bacteria!

- And believe it or not (but this is true), there's a type of food people love in Sardinia called *casu marzu*. It is made by flies laying their eggs in cheese, then the maggot babies hatch and slowly chomp and poo out the stuff till it's ready to serve … I'm genuinely sorry if I've just put you off cheese sandwiches for life.

I pulled myself up in a frenzy, grabbing any slimy surface I could to get out of this stinky mess. My fingers slipped through decomposing food, but every now and then I managed to find something hard that I could heave myself a bit further up from. Eventually, I saw light and I could just make out Liam's voice shouting at Clio for help.

Before I knew what was happening, I felt the squeeze

of my sister's fingers tight around me as she pulled me out to safety and plonked me on the floor.

I lay there, staring at the ceiling, gasping in great mouthfuls of delicious fresh air. Liam's face appeared and he checked my pulse like we were in a movie.

'Do you need me to give you mouth-to-mouth resuscitation?' he asked, seriously.

'No, I didn't drown, I'm not dead,' I said. 'Just … traumatized.' I sat up quickly before he could try out the CPR first aid training he'd done at Cubs, and he pulled something sticky off my forehead, which ended up being a squashed pea. I looked down at my clothes — I was absolutely filthy.

'Here you go,' said Liam warmly, and he pulled off the army outfit and offered it to me. I yanked off my revolting clothes and pulled on the only-slightly-less-disgusting costume (it *had* been in a nappy bin, after all), but it was dry and it hadn't come into contact with maggots.

'You look good! That suits you. You look like you're

straight out of that combat battle simulator game!' Liam grinned, handing me the plastic gun. I slid it into my belt.

'Cheers, Liam,' I grinned.

'Come on,' he said smiling back. 'Let's see if we've cracked riddle two and levelled up.'

FRIDAY AFTERNOON, 5.48 P.M.

COUNTDOWN TIMER: 9 MINUTES

LIVES: 1/3

hrinkle's cat purred, 'Congratulations!' (but he didn't sound like he meant it). 'It took you rather a long time, but you solved my second little puzzle. Now for my final *rrrr* … riddle. Find, if you can: what has a head, a tail, but no body?'

'What could that be?' I asked. 'A clock has hands … A table has legs …'

'A comb has teeth,' Liam shrugged.

'Right, but what has no body ... a skeleton?'

Only this morning, Liam had told a (terrible) joke about the skeleton having NO BODY to go to the party with as we'd fought over a box of Coco Pops. (We'd ended up in a tug of war and the last of the cereal had ended up on the floor. Clio or Declan had probably cleared it up — and by that, I mean wolfed it down along with fluff and whatever else you might find on the kitchen floor.)

How could that possibly have been THIS MORNING? The day had started off so normally and now look at us ... I felt like we'd been tiny forever — and that was beyond freaky, of course. But equally as bizarre was that Liam and I were kind of **getting on**. He'd saved my life ... more than once. And, I had to admit, it was better when he was around. He's always so optimistic. Liam's cup is not just half full, it's overflowing — which normally drives me bonkers, but when you're faced with near-certain doom and only seven centimetres tall, it's quite heartening.

'Maybe it's one of Clio's weird cuddly toys?' he suggested.

I swear, in her cot, Clio has:

- A soft toy called 'Sheldon the shrimp' that she takes *everywhere*. Sheldon is literally a cuddly shrimp — a shrimp! Perhaps the least loveable thing in the universe. Who'd choose to snuggle a shrimp?
- A velvet BROCCOLI toy, with googly eyes. (What sort of deranged toy manufacturer decided that a vegetable would make a cute toy?)
- Thinking hard about it, she also had a strange dog-type thing she called 'Poopy-time', which was really all head and tail, with no proper body shape at all. (Clio once accidentally dropped Poopy-time over the side of a boat. She cried so hard and made such a fuss that the captain

thought Poopy-time was a *real* pet and made an emergency stop to rescue it from the River Thames. Clio couldn't care less about Poopy-time now and didn't even mind that Poopy-time had become Dec's favourite toy. Dec spent his limited waking hours clawing at it or carrying it to her in his mouth.)

Could it really be Poopy-time that Shrinkle was asking us to find? How could Shrinkle possibly know about Poopy-time? Shrinkle was a game, downloaded from the internet. It couldn't know the precise objects in our flat … Could it?

'Wait! It's not a toy. I've got it! It's a coin!' shrieked Liam. 'Think about it, it has a head on one side, a tail on the other … and no body!'

'Liam, you're a genius!' I exclaimed. (I know, I know, I said he wasn't a genius and I stand by that, but at that very moment, he was thinking like a genius.)

Shrinkle's cat snarled unhappily and the sand timer popped up on the screen.

'We've only got eight minutes left!' I screeched. 'Where's a coin?'

'I tripped over one under my bed,' Liam grinned.

'There's not enough time to run back to our room and what if we can't find it in the dark?' My chest began to heave with the stress.

'Well, how about I try and hack into Shrinkle's code?' Liam said, raising an eyebrow. He spends hours programming his own games. Maybe it was possible he could just insert 'coin' into the correct place in the software script and we'd win the game — just like that —and it would all be over? It would surely less of a risk then running into that spider again.

Switching from the user control interface to lines and lines of data, Liam attempted to find the right bit of computer text.

'Hang on, here's the code for the stats page,' Liam

grinned. 'Just think about it: I could alter it all! I could give us more strength or intelligence. What if I gave us the ability to fly! We don't even need to crack the riddle — I could just adjust our height in the code, so we'll be back to normal size!'

I felt sick with worry as I watched my brother scanning the code.

'We might end up the right height, but lose our density? What if we end up tall enough but stay one centimetre wide, like strands of human spaghetti? Or we might just float in air, our heads at the right height but with our bodies not reaching the ground. Liam, don't take any risks.'

'Hang on,' he said, 'it says here we've only got ONE life left. How did …?'

My face began to flush red.

'Okay, okay. It's all good! Ha! I've found the third riddle code,' he grinned and I let out a sigh of relief. 'Let me just make sure I insert it into the correct place …'

and he typed 'coin' carefully into the phone.

The reward crown icon flashed up and a chiming sound rang out …

We'd done it! We'd solved the riddles. But then the crown quickly disappeared and Shrinkle's cat filled the screen, his eyes glowing menacingly red and looking ferocious. He began twitching and hissed, '*Cheaters!* I don't like cheaters. How dare you hack into my code. You may have cracked my final riddle, but NOW you have to fight the BOSS and find the key to unlock the game. And just to warn you, I don't like being beaten.'

'Oww!' Liam yelped, springing away from the phone. 'The case — it's burning hot!'

A thick trail of smoke began billowing out of the battery compartment.

'The phone is overheating,' I cried. 'Shrinkle, how do we beat the boss? Tell us what to do!'

'Well,' cackled the cat, 'you've got all the answers. Can't you work it out? Think about the riddles, what letters did you uncover?'

'Um … Do you mean the letter at the beginning of each answer? The first one was dictionary — so D?' I wracked my brains, trying to remember all the objects we'd found while simultaneously trying to suppress pure panic from overwhelming me. 'Er, E for egg. Then C … for coin. D-E-C? Dec?' I said confused. 'What does that mean? Do you mean … Declan? Miss McBoob's cat? Dec is the baddy boss!'

I laughed out loud with relief. Dec is literally the laziest, softest-hearted cat you could ever imagine. He wouldn't hurt a mouse if it stole his dinner. Or if it was snoozing in his bed. He'd probably lend it his duvet. (If cats had duvets.)

'Find Dec's special key and you've won the game!' Shrinkle's cat purred intensely. Then the image began to glitch, and without warning the glass screen suddenly shattered into fragments.

Liam and I both jumped back.

'We need to find Dec,' I screeched and Liam nodded vigorously. I hadn't seen Dec since he'd been asleep on Miss McBoob's lap and he definitely hadn't been there when I'd almost fallen down her slimy pink throat. We'd been in practically every room of the flat during the last hour. Could he have gone home? *But the front door has been closed the entire time,* I realized.

What if he'd climbed through a window?

What if we couldn't find him in time?

Suddenly a shadow fell across the room. I spun around and looked at the doorway.

Dec stood, towering above us, impossibly tall and intimidating on his hind legs. On his head there was the strange metal hat that had fallen out of Miss McBoob's bag. It seemed locked onto Dec's head and an unnerving, pulsating light flashed at the top.

'Dec …?' I stuttered, holding onto Liam for support as my legs turned to jelly.

Behind us, I could hear Shrinkle's cat laughing wildly.

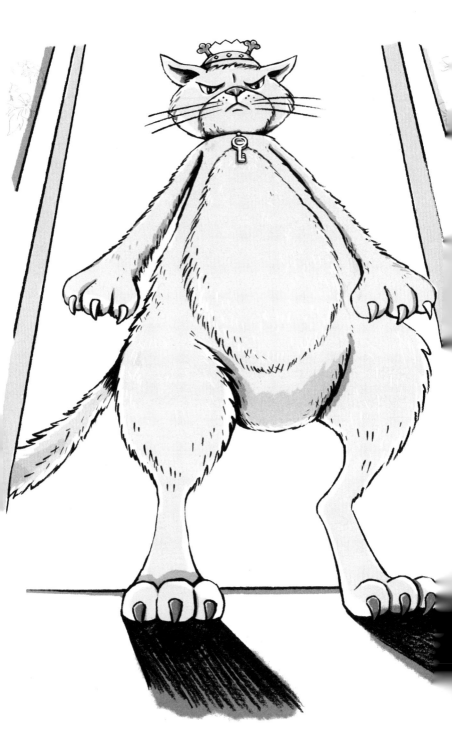

'What do you think of Dec's new look? Glamorous, huh? That's a mind control helmet on his head, in case you were wondering. I can control his brain activity. Dec's on my side now.'

'Dec, it's us! Max and Liam,' I called up to him. Dec starred at us blankly. Then laser beams shot out of his eyes, scorching great big burn holes into the carpet.

I leapt back, pulling Liam with me. I couldn't speak. Dec glided his head round robotically to face us and fired again. We sprang away, as the carpet took another hit and two more smouldering craters appeared.

'We've got to get out of here!' Liam screamed and he pulled me towards Dec.

'What are you doing?' I cried, but Liam yanked me right through Dec's legs and we bolted, half tripping down the hallway.

'Don't … look … back,' he cried, between gasping for breaths. 'Let's … find … somewhere … to … hide … and … come … up … with … a … plan.'

We dashed into the kitchen, Liam limping badly, and we both skidded behind the dustpan.

Clio had deserted the terrible mix of food from the fridge and was nowhere to be seen.

'What's happened to Dec? How can the game have done this to him?' Liam stuttered. 'What do we do?'

'I think we've got to touch the tag around Dec's neck,' I whispered. 'It's got Dec's name engraved on it and it's in the shape of a little key. Shrinkle's cat said *find Dec's special key, and we've won the game.*

'Okay, but how are we possibly going to reach it without getting laser beamed to death?' he asked.

Just then, we heard a whirring noise and to our utter terror and amazement, Liam's remote control car drove itself into the kitchen, the phone still on top.

LEVEL TEN

FRIDAY AFTERNOON, 5.53 P.M.

COUNTDOWN TIMER: 4 MINUTES

LIVES: 1/3

hrinkle's cat sniggered. 'Ah, little boys ... You thought you could outrun me. How sweet.'

'What have you done to Dec?' I choked out as the kitchen lights began to flicker.

'Oh, that was simple!' snorted Shrinkle's cat. 'You see, I'm a very exceptional piece of software. I can tap into the electric forces of everything around me. All I have to do is spark currents in the atoms of Dec's eyes and that creates beams of energy. Deadly beams! I don't think your plastic gun will be much use against them, do you?'

Eyes wide, I glanced up as the microwave began pinging aggressively. At the same time, Mum's blender whirred into action. The metal blades were slashing too fast and sparks of energy shot off in different directions. The microwave door suddenly sprang open, shoving the blender off the shelf so that it toppled to the ground with an almighty **smash**.

Stunned, we watched in silence, our mouths gaping open as the electric tin opener noisily ripped off the lid of a tin of baked beans and the toaster made an urgent buzzing noise.

An electric cackle erupted and a slice of toast blasted out, flying through the air and crash-landing centimetres from where we were crouching. Crumbs as a big as bullets ricocheted towards us.

We ducked down, only *just* escaping their blow.

I felt for Liam's hand and gripped it tightly. It was cold and clammy, just like mine. Soapy suds began to leak from the dishwasher and a puddle spread quickly across the floor, edging towards us, carrying remnants of Clio's revolting food concoction. We climbed frantically on top of the dustpan, but as more filthy dishwater gushed out of the machine, I realized … *we were moving*! The dustpan was being carried away with the current and we had no choice but to hang on for our lives.

We were swept out into the hallway.

The car was already ahead of us. Shrinkle had reversed out of the kitchen and was driving back towards Mum's room.

'We've got to get to Dec's collar. *Fast!*' I said. But I didn't know how. Shrinkle was now in control of all the electrical appliances in the flat.

We didn't stand a chance.

Liam was really beginning to panic. His bottom lip was trembling and he'd gone as white as sheet. 'We can do this,' I said. 'I need you. Shrinkle's just a game and we're great at games. Remember that time last summer when we beat Dad at penalty shoot-out?'

(It had been incredible. Dad is a surprisingly good goalkeeper and I'd never managed to get a ball past him before. He'd bet us unlimited Monster Shakes at the new cafe on the main street if we won, and even with stakes that high we'd somehow pulled it off. We'd dined on the creamiest, most decadent shakes every day after school for the entire year.)

Liam gave me a brave smile and we slipped off the dustpan, our feet skidding over the wet floorboards.

Dec was still standing on his hind legs in Mum's bedroom doorway. He turned round to look at us, his eyes bright red. From behind him, I could make out Shrinkle's cat howling with laughter, but the sound was quickly drowned out by the hum of Mum's super power-ful vacuum cleaner. If we didn't do something soon, we would get SUCKED UP …

'Okay, so what's the plan?' Liam asked, looking at me expectantly. I glanced around for inspiration. Clio was oblivious to our crisis and was singing loudly in her bedroom, throwing her toys high into the air.

Suddenly, I saw Poopy-time hurled skywards.

'Poopy-time!' I yelled gleefully.

'NOW? Are you serious?' Liam asked.

'Clio's toy! Dec is crazy about it!' I explained. 'Come on!'

Helping Liam hobble to Clio's room, we stealthily grabbed Poopy-time and rolled it towards the hall.

'Right, you distract Dec,' I said, desperately willing that some part of him would still recognize his favourite toy. 'And I'll … um, climb onto Dec's back and get to the key …' I didn't sound very convincing.

Liam looked doubtful, but the low drone of the vacuum cleaner was getting louder. Suddenly my battery-operated pirate figure appeared from our bedroom and marched towards us, slashing his super sharp sword through the air. His silver cloak flapped majestically as my toy drone hovered above him. Perched on top was Clio's electronic shark bath toy, who seemed to be pelting us with … baked beans.

'Now!' I yelled, and made a run for Dec. He shot laser beams at me and I leapt hastily out of the way.

An army of cat fleas, each as big as a mouse, seemed to spawn from Dec's fur and sprang towards me. I could hear Liam shout, 'Dec, look! It's Poopy-time,' as I kept running, determination pumping through my veins. I swatted off the vicious-looking fleas with the plastic gun and didn't stop charging forward.

Dec twisted his head to look at Liam and suddenly flopped down onto all four legs. The plan was working! He crouched down, ready to spring for Poopy-time. I wouldn't have another chance. I didn't freeze this time. I climbed onto Dec's tail, grabbing fistfuls of cat fur and hauled myself up onto his back. My heart was racing and sweat poured down my forehead, but I scrambled

upwards as quickly as I could. I'd almost reached his collar. I stretched out my arm as far as I could …

Suddenly Dec leapt forward to grab Poopy-time. Gritting my teeth, I clenched my fingers around his fur as we soared through the air.

'Max!' Liam shouted, letting go of Poopy-time and rolling sideways as Dec slashed his sharp claws into the soft toy.

Somehow, I'd managed to hold on. Panting for breath, I reached forward and held my hand steadily on the glittering key around Dec's neck.

'Dec!' I hollered as loud as I could.

The mind control helmet exploded violently and a flash of blinding light filled the hall. Instinctively I slammed my eyes shut.

I could feel myself changing … decompacting … like a spring loaded, pop-up tent being released from its bag and expanding, *poof*, to full size.

'**Yeeeeoooowwww!**' A growl erupted. *Was that*

Shrinkle's cat? I snapped open my eyes and realized the sound was coming from my bum — I was sitting ON Dec.

I leapt off him … I was big again!

I blinked uncontrollably, trying to make sense of what had just happened. The flat looked unbelievably tiny.

I glanced around, looking for Liam. He was sitting on the floor by the kitchen, surrounded by dirty dishwater, grinning ecstatically. I ran towards him and threw my arms around my brother in utter relief and joy.

'We've done it … We've won the game!' I cried, a tear rolling down my cheek.

'Ooh, is my little pussykins okay? I heard him meow,' Miss McBoob cooed, rubbing her eyes sleepily as she stumbled out of the living room and picked up Dec.

He drooped himself around Miss McBoob's shoulders and began purring loudly. The mind control helmet lay shattered on the floor amongst our (thankfully still) electronic toys. Within an instant, Dec began snoring loudly.

Just then, we heard the key rattle in the lock as Mum arrived home. She stared at us all in disbelief.

'What's going on?' she asked slowly, taking in the utter carnage of the flat.

She marched into Clio's room and held my baby sister up, checked her all over then squeezed her tightly to her chest.

'Sharky fire baked beans!' Clio said, smiling. 'And liddle Maxy and liddle Liam not tiny no more.'

'Er … Have you been playing make believe with your brothers?' Mum asked. Clio shook her head but Mum ignored her as she looked at us in confusion, sitting on the floor together, surrounded by water and grinning wildly.

'Has there been an electrical fault in the flat? Or a leak? It looks like both,' Mum spluttered. 'Are you all okay?'

'We're all right now, Mum. It's all good!' I replied, squeezing Liam's shoulder.

As we all helped clear up the mess, Mum began smiling in a goofy kind of way. 'You know who I bumped into on the way home? Aimi Tanaka!'

'So?' I said, instantly blushing bright red.

'You know, Min Tanaka's mum. Apparently, Min has a crush on you! She talks about you all the time!'

'Stop it, Mum,' I said, my cheeks burning. 'You must have got that wrong.' And I sped out of the kitchen to avoid anything else horrifically embarrassing Mum might say.

There's no way that could be true? Min … like me? Ridiculous.

Eventually we crashed on the sofa and Mum brought out a platter of the tiny food that she'd made for the cancelled party. I couldn't quite look at it, it was just so small. Only an hour ago, those hamburgers would have been XXL size.

I wasn't sure I'd ever be able to look at anything in the same way again. Especially Liam. I didn't know why I'd

always been so mad at him. He'd only ever been himself. Yes, he was full-on and reckless. But that also made him fun and fearless. And maybe he wasn't always trying to put me down or wind me up ... Maybe I'd been seeing it wrong the whole time.

'So ...' Mum said slowly. 'Do you want the bad news or the good news first?'

'Er ...' I hesitated.

'Well,' Mum said, 'the bad news is, it turns out, you were right, Liam.'

Liam looked totally baffled.

'There was an incident with the school chef. Mr Flambét was ... um... cutting corners and has admitted to putting some ... er, objectionable meat into the school lunches. Mr Flambét has been fired and will never work in the catering industry again.'

Liam and I looked at each other, stunned.

'So I guess you're not in trouble. The headteacher says he admires your bravery in being a whistleblower and so … your screen ban is over. And seeing as you two seem to be getting along, here are all your devices.' Mum unzipped a large bag, revealing all our treasured wires, tablets and keyboards that she'd stripped from the flat before she left.

'So what's the good news?' Liam said with excitement. 'I mean the bad news was pretty awesome!'

'Well,' said Mum brightly, 'the school needs a new chef! I'm being interviewed for the position on Monday morning! Imagine, if I get the job I'll see you at school every day!'

This was a level ten disaster. Our Mum, the new school dinner lady, checking up on us at every chance …

'And Max, your dad was at the meeting with the head teacher tonight, too.'

I stared at Dad's empty leather chair and then down at my feet.

'We both saw your "The Evolution of the Video Game" display in the hall. It's amazing.'

'It's not finished.' I said quickly.

'Well, your dad told me to tell you, he is so **proud** of you.'

I bit my bottom lip.

'He misses you so much, Max. He's really hoping you'll meet him for a milkshake with Clio and Liam tomorrow. Will you go?'

'Please come, Max. It'd be so much better if you were there,' Liam said.

'I'll think about it,' I said, giving him a secret little smile.

'Right, well, I think I'd better be off home now,' Miss McBoob said, smiling and popping the last mini hamburger into her mouth. 'I've got things to be getting on with. Before I leave, has anybody seen my mobile telephone? I seem to have misplaced it.' she said, scooping up Dec from the sofa.

I gulped nervously.

'Nope? Never mind, I'm always losing it. I'm working

on a new portable telephone device anyway, with a frequency that can pick up signals from distant galaxies,' she exclaimed, strolling out of our flat. 'Toodle-oo dears.'

'Er, we'll just be in our room,' I blurted, grabbing Liam by the hand for a full, brother-to-brother debrief.

The End

(… for now)